MW00961895

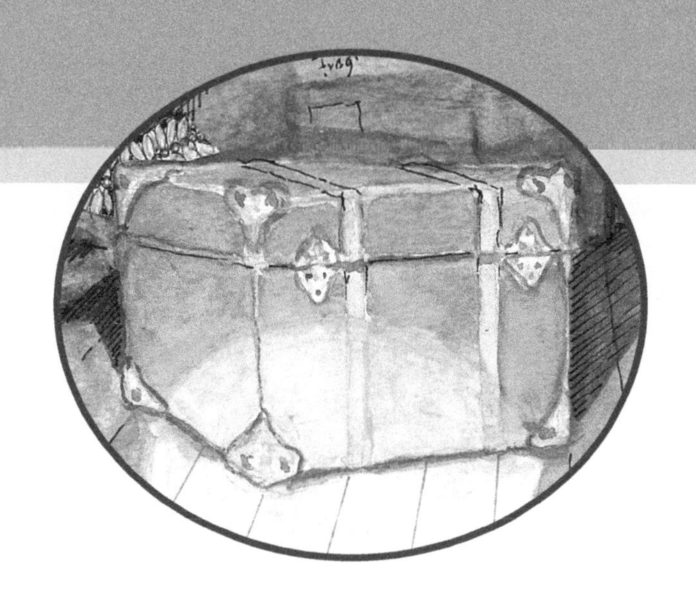

Treasure in the Trunk

A wordless picture book by

Linda MacRitchie Graf

BOOM
STEAMER TRUNK

WOW !

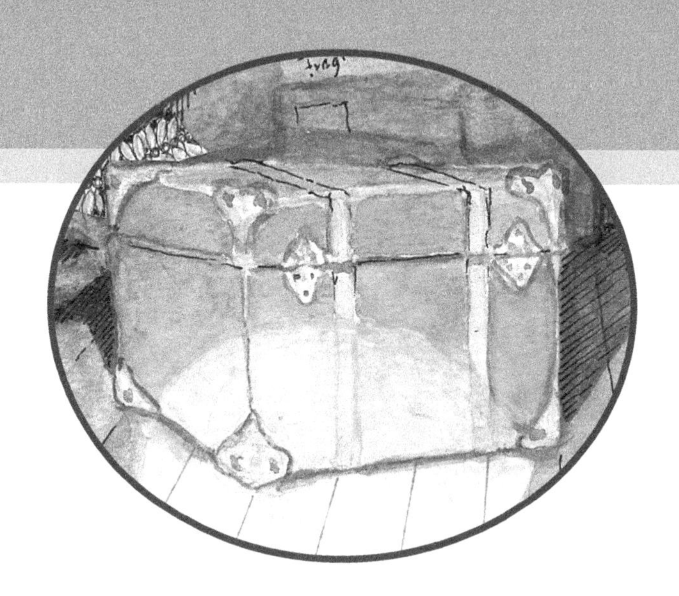

A wordless picture book by
Linda MacRitchie Graf

Buffalo Heritage Press
266 Elmwood Avenue, Suite 407
Buffalo, New York 14222
www.BuffaloHeritage.com

ISBN: 978-1-942483-67-0 (softcover)
ISBN: 978-1-942483-68-7 (hardcover)

Library of Congress control number available upon request.

Printed in the United States of America.

CPSIA information can be obtained
at www.ICGtesting.com
Printed in the USA
LVHW012309250719
625402LV00002B/4/P

9 781942 483687